NIGHTMARE
AT SKULL JUNCTION

WORD _Kids!_

WORD PUBLISHING
Dallas · London · Vancouver · Melbourne

NIGHTMARE AT SKULL JUNCTION

Copyright © 1992 by Roger Elwood.

Editor: Beverly Phillips

Library of Congress Cataloging-in-Publication Data

Elwood, Roger.
    Nightmare at Skull Junction / Roger Elwood.
       p.   cm.—(Bartlett brothers)
    "Word kids"
    Summary: Teenage brothers Chad and Ryan help their father
uncover a deadly plot to force Indians living near a mining operation in
the Mojave Desert off their land.
    ISBN 0–8499–3361–7
    [1. Christian life—Fiction. 2. Indians of North America—
Southwest, New—Fiction. 3. Adventure and adventurers—
Fiction. 4. Criminals—Fiction. 5. Brothers—Fiction.] I. Title.
II. Series: Elwood, Roger. Bartlett brothers.
PZ7.E554Ni   1992
[Fic]—dc20   92–7295
                                                    CIP
                                                     AC

Printed in the United States of America

2 3 4 5 6 7 8 9   RRD   9 8 7 6 5 4 3 2 1

To
Diane Dixon
—for love returned

Acknowledgments

Nightmare at Skull Junction is the sixth novel in the Bartlett Brothers series. Young people are reading these books but so are many of their parents who like what I am trying to accomplish with these books.

None of this could be happening if it weren't for Laura Minchew at Word Publishing and, also, Joey Paul. They have stood firm by their belief in my writing, and my life as well as my career are enriched in a number of ways as a result.

But let me add several other individuals: Lee Gessner, whose sales team has done such an extraordinary job in selling the series; Beverly Phillips, whose editing can only be called a tremendous asset; and Dave Moberg, Byron Williamson, and Charles "Kip" Jordon for supporting those who are supporting me. They all have my support, my very best efforts.

I do not forget the readers, the many thousands who have responded to the Bartlett Brothers with such enthusiasm—along with the bookstore managers, the distributors, and others without whom there would be no continuing series.

God bless you all. . . .

Roger Elwood

 **One**

The black plastic walkie-talkie, its antenna slightly bent, was lying in the desert with an arrow partially buried in the sand next to it.

As Chad Bartlett brought the large Yamaha motorcycle to a stop beside it, his brother Ryan and he got off to examine such a puzzling find in the middle of the Mojave desert.

"Real strange," Chad said as he picked up the walkie-talkie. "I wonder if it still works."

He pressed the send button, and said "Hello" several times into the built-in microphone.

"Hey, where have you been?" a harsh-sounding voice asked at the other end. "You haven't run into any members of the tribe, have you? You're not letting those savages scare you off? In a few months, we won't have to worry at all. They'll be dead, the entire tribe. You know that as well as I. Do what you're supposed to and get the devil back here!"

Chad almost dropped the device as those words made it through a high level of static and other interference.

"What's going on?" the voice continued, more frantic this time. "Is that you or someone—?"

The connection was broken as soon as the individual at the other end realized he might have been talking to a stranger.

They'll be dead, the entire tribe. The words were still ringing in Chad's ears.

"Did you hear that, Ryan? It sounds like some kind of murder plot."

Ryan nodded, though the idea seemed bizarre.

"An entire tribe slated for extermination!" he exclaimed. "It sounds crazy. But still, we should head back into town and alert Dad."

"Agreed," Chad told him. "Praise God that Dad's with us this time. That hasn't always been the case."

He quickly stuffed the walkie-talkie into a leather pouch hanging down the side of the cycle.

As they were starting to leave that spot, rifle fire rang out.

Several bullets hit the sand around them, one *zinged* off the cycle's black metal side.

"Wait or run for it?" Chad asked.

"If we wait, and whoever it is catches us, what will they do to us?" Ryan added. "Let's try running."

"You're right. I can't believe they'll actually try to kill us. In fact, what in the world did we do to get them mad at us in the first place?"

"Could it be what we just heard over the walkie-talkie? You know, that's probably it, Chad."

"We're outtahere!" his brother agreed.

Chad gunned the motorcycle forward, as fast as the powerful motor would take them.

For a minute or two, there was no more shooting.

An explosion instead.

"A grenade!" Chad shouted above the sudden blast of noise.

A short distance ahead of them, the device had exploded in a cloud of sand.

Chad veered the cycle to the left and saw something that he wished he hadn't about a half a mile ahead.

A jeep.

Heading straight toward them.

"They *won't* get us!" Chad declared, swinging around one hundred and eighty degrees away from the jeep.

The motor stalled, bringing the cycle to an abrupt halt and both boys went flying off.

"We're sunk," Ryan muttered. "We're—."

His words were cut off as another grenade exploded just a few yards away. They were surrounded by a mini sandstorm.

"I don't hear the jeep!" Chad yelled.

"I don't either," Ryan added. "Where did they go?"

A second or two later, they saw the jeep lying on its side. The wheels were still spinning.

The brothers exchanged glances.

"Let's get away from this spot as fast as we can," Chad remarked, perspiration dripping down his forehead and onto his cheeks.

"But what happened?" Ryan asked.

"Hey, I don't know. I just know they're not going to be chasing us anymore."

Ryan squinted.

"Look at the left front tire on the jeep," he said.

"Another arrow!" Chad observed.

Ryan started walking toward the jeep.

He didn't have to go far before he discovered that both men had been killed, probably by concussions or other internal damage when the vehicle rolled over on its side.

Two more large arrows, apparently designed to travel an exceptionally long distance were sticking out of the front seat.

"Old idea, new technology," Ryan said in real amazement. "Those arrows look something like miniature rockets, don't you think, not the plain ones used in the old days."

"Where did they come from?" Chad mused.

"There's your answer," said Ryan, pointing north toward five palomino horses, ridden by men in full Indian battle dress! *Oh, Lord,* he said to himself, *I wish Dad were here right now.*

# Two

Andrew Bartlett was standing before a window in his hotel room at the Sagebrush Inn, which was an authentically recreated 1870s-era building in an authentically recreated Western town of the same period.

This assignment was not the usual sort of mission for the National Security Advisor to the President of the United States.

He was there on official business all right, but not the kind that required any emergency help, including security for himself and his sons. And as far as Chad and Ryan were concerned, it seemed very much like their dad was on a working vacation. For Andrew Bartlett, having the boys with him made his presence much less intimidating because the trip would seem less formal.

I told them what was happening, he thought. *I said that it was unlikely there would be any danger. The only reason for going in a rather casual manner was to get genuine insight into the problem, not remarks for so-called political effect, things that people say to look good or to avoid looking bad.*

Indians were dying.

The death rate among the inhabitants on the reservation nearby had shot up by a huge percentage over the past two years.

"Something's going on, Andy," the president had told him last week as they both sat in the Oval Office.

"What do you suppose it might be, Mr. President?"

"Pollution of some sort. It's all started since mining companies moved in all around the reservation."

"Violations of codes guaranteed to protect the tribe's rights in such circumstances?" Mr. Bartlett asked.

"I cannot say for sure, but at the moment, I just do not see any other reasonable possibilities."

"Are *all* the companies involved, Mr. President?"

"I doubt it."

"Any suspicions, Mr. President?"

"I have not a single clue, Andy, not a one. You know, it always amazes me when any American

8

company places the health and survival of human lives on a lower level than profits."

"Safety standards cost money."

"That's right, Andy. Just proves once again how right the apostle Paul was when he wrote about the love of money being the root of all evil. You and I have seen enough *evidence* of that over the years."

Mr. Bartlett nodded.

"You're reading the Bible more these days, Mr. President?"

"Just like I promised I would, Andy. We'll talk about that after you return from your trip out West."

"I'm looking forward to doing so, Mr. President."

"So am I, Andy, so am I."

When Chad and Ryan had returned home on that last day of the school year, Mr. Bartlett told them about the trip.

They both were excited.

"There's all sorts of caves out there," Ryan said. "It's a place of legends. Skull Junction could be real fun."

Chad agreed.

"I can hardly wait, Dad," he said.

Since the two of them were just beginning their summer vacation, they would have plenty of time on their hands. Neither of them was due to start their part-time jobs for a couple of weeks.

"It should be pretty routine stuff as far as *my* work is concerned," Mr. Bartlett said honestly.

"But why is the president sending you, then, Dad?" Ryan asked an obvious question.

"Because, frankly, son, there are no real international crises boiling over just now. After I get back, though, I think the president has in mind something to do with the war on drugs."

"Not the Forbidden River Cartel again?" Chad put in, remembering all too well the nightmarish series of experiences that had threatened to take the lives of all three of them.

"I doubt it," his father replied. "Their attempts to corrupt government officials last year did them more harm than good. Public outrage was so intense that the politicians voted more money than any of us could ever have imagined to fund a direct assault against the Cartel."

"It was fantastic, Dad!" Ryan exclaimed. "The South Americans really cooperated, despite all those threats against them and their families. Several of the drug bosses were captured, their processing labs destroyed."

"But the main honcho escaped," Mr. Bartlett reminded him. "It might be that he's set up shop elsewhere."

Whatever awaited Andrew Bartlett after he returned from the trip West, he was glad to have the opportunity of getting away with his sons.

The phone rang, snapping him out of his reflections.

It was a man named Robert Claiborne.

"I am very pleased that you have arrived at last, Mr. Bartlett," Claiborne remarked in a voice that seemed friendly, but in a put-on manner.

"It would be fine if you called me Andy, sir."

"Only if you call me Bob."

"Good! When do you want to meet?" Andrew Bartlett asked.

There was only the slightest hesitation.

"How about this afternoon at 4:00?"

"Fine," Mr. Bartlett agreed heartily. "My sons Chad and Ryan won't be back until after six o'clock. So I'm free till then. They're out doing a little exploring on some astonishing new off-road motorcycle that they found for rent in a local bike shop."

"Were they headed to any special point of interest?" Claiborne asked, the tone of his voice changing a bit.

"Indeed they were, Bob. They said they intended to check out the site of the original Skull Junction near the reservation. I think they're

11

hoping to find a ghost town or an old cave. You know how boys are."

Silence.

For a moment, Mr. Bartlett thought the line had gone dead.

"Bob, Bob?" he repeated. "Are you still there?"

"I am . . ." the voice came back on the line. "We are truly still out in the sticks here, I must admit, Andy. Sometimes the phone lines do prove to be, shall we say, most unreliable. Sorry about that."

"No problem."

"I'm afraid your boys are going to be disappointed. There's not much to see out there, maybe a few shabby Indian huts. Say, I'll send a car to pick you up at 3:45. Or is that too early?"

"Just right. Thanks, Bob."

"Good. I'll see you at 4:00."

Click.

Before his present job as National Security Advisor, Andy Bartlett had spent many years as a spy, working undercover as an employee of the State Department. He had developed a set of what might be called special mental antennae that vibrated when something was wrong. This sixth sense had served him well for a very long time, even to the point of saving his life more than once.

There was something strange about the conversation he'd just completed with Bob Claiborne. That long silence . . .

For a moment, Mr. Bartlett thought the line had gone dead.

"Bob, Bob?" he repeated. "Are you still there?"

Andrew Bartlett's palms were sweating.

I told Chad and Ryan what was happening. . . . I said that it was unlikely there would be any danger.

Dear Lord, I pray that I wasn't wrong.

 # Three

After dismounting the palominos, the five Indians quickly surrounded Chad and Ryan.

"My name is Brook-That-Sings," one of them said. "Why are you on our land?"

"We have no reason," answered Chad, "except we were doing a little sightseeing and I was trying out a motorcycle that looked real good."

"That one?" Brook-That-Sings said, as he pointed with some admiration at the black bike.

Chad nodded.

"It is very fine looking."

"Thank you."

"We saw you being chased by the men in the jeep. What did you do to make them want to harm you?"

"We stumbled across a walkie-talkie in the sand with an arrow next to it," Ryan replied. "And we overheard a message that—"

He cut himself off.

"What was the message?" Brook-That-Sings asked.

"It was . . . was . . . well, I . . . I—," Ryan stuttered nervously.

"What is your name?"

"Ryan . . . Ryan Bartlett."

"And yours?" he asked, turning to Chad.

"Chad Bartlett."

"You two have nothing to fear from us. I ask about the message because the man carrying that walkie-talkie was sent here to see how much poison had seeped into our water and the land we've reclaimed from this sandy desert."

"What's wrong with that?" Ryan asked.

"I did not finish," Brook-That-Sings told him.

"Sorry . . ." Ryan said, embarrassed.

"He came to check the level of contamination, only to see if his people needed to make it higher!"

"You're saying that these guys are deliberately doing this?" Chad asked disbelievingly.

"For two years now," the Indian commented.

"I guess we should tell you, then, something we heard over the walkie-talkie," Chad added with some discomfort.

"Yes, it would be good if you did this," Brook-That-Sings acknowledged. "It might be another piece in the puzzle that my people have been trying to put together for so long now."

Chad repeated what the harsh-sounding voice had said: *"You're not letting those savages scare you off, are you? In a few months we won't have to worry at all. They'll be dead, the entire tribe. You know that as well as I. Do what you're supposed to and get the devil back here."*

Instantly, upon hearing that, Brook-That-Sings and the others fell to their knees, and bowed their heads.

"They're praying," Ryan whispered to his brother.

"I can tell," Chad replied.

Their common prayer, spoken in the Indians' native language, lasted for several minutes.

When the small group of Indians finally stood, Brook-That-Sings could see that Chad and Ryan were surprised.

"Not all native Americans worship strange gods," he said pointedly.

"We didn't—," Chad started to say.

"You didn't have to. Your faces reveal more than you might realize."

Brook-That-Sings smiled broadly.

"We also sense how honest you and your brother are. We feel that we can trust you."

"Maybe we could help," Ryan offered.

"It would take a great deal, Ryan Bartlett," remarked Brook-That-Sings, with deep weariness, his expression suggesting that there was no way he could guess that two white teenagers could ever be of meaningful help to a desperate group of Native Americans who were slowly dying.

"We could tell our father," Chad put in.

"And what could your father do, my new friend?" the Indian replied kindly, but in a doubting manner that reflected a lifetime of disappointments.

Chad went on to tell him where Andrew Bartlett worked and what his job was.

Brook-That-Sings and his fellow Indians immediately dropped to their knees again.

"Let's join them this time," said Ryan in a low voice.

Chad nodded.

Within a few seconds, strangers had joined hands in the middle of the desert, each one praying in earnest.

Ryan and Chad knew if they could only reach their father that he would be able to find some way to help these Indians.

 **Four**

Robert Claiborne was quite tall and quite bald. He looked like a combination of President Dwight Eisenhower and the wrestler King Kong Bundy.

Claiborne's office in a stucco-fronted building on the outskirts of Skull Junction was as plush as any Andrew Bartlett had seen, with expensive cherrywood paneling, a desk made of the same kind of wood, and light beige carpeting so thick that shoes tended to sink down into it well above the sole.

"Please, sit down," Claiborne said, indicating a leather-covered chair in front of that massive, hand-carved desk.

"You have done very well, I see," Mr. Bartlett observed, as he glanced over the rest of the office. The suspended ceiling was made of top-of-the-line tiles patterned with gold flecks. The built-in technically-advanced stereo system had two large symphonic speakers in each of the four corners.

A carved oak liquor cabinet was stocked with rare wines. And the wall was covered with gold-plated frames containing award certificates and photos of Claiborne with American presidents, British prime ministers, and other famous individuals.

"The results of a lifetime," Claiborne said with obvious pride. "We are the sum total of that which we accumulate in one way or another, of one sort or another. Wouldn't you agree, Andy?"

"Actually I wouldn't," Mr. Bartlett told him honestly.

"How come? You seem intelligent, Andy. How *could* you possibly disagree with what I've said?"

"Material possessions are often, I should say, quite meaningless when it comes to life-or-death issues."

"But they show what we have accomplished. A man who has a Jaguar parked in his driveway is obviously more successful than someone who is driving around in a three-year-old Chevrolet."

"I disagree, Bob. I have known wealthy men who didn't want to parade around their status, so they took the Chevy or the Ford or the Olds instead. But I have also been acquainted with men who bought their Jaguars, their Mercedes, or their Porsches on credit and, later, due to business reversals, ended up in bankruptcy court."

He cleared his throat, then added, "The Bible reveals a great deal about material possessions being the downfall of the human soul much more than any possible blessing they might offer."

"The Bible is not to be a topic of discussion," Claiborne said, his irritation showing. "I'm surprised you would mention it since you are here as a representative of the President of the United States."

"You mean the separation of church and state, that sort of thing, Bob?" Mr. Bartlett asked.

"That's precisely what I mean, Andy."

"I didn't happen to be offering you any sort of a national policy statement but, rather, merely a personal opinion."

"Then keep your opinions to yourself!"

"Where is your friendliness now, Bob?"

"Where your views about God and the Bible should have been placed before you entered this office."

Mr. Bartlett waited a moment before answering. He had learned not to lose his temper while he was on the government's time.

"I suggest we start discussing why I *am* here," he said.

"You mean the deaths of those savages?"

Mr. Bartlett's face flushed at that remark.

"I wouldn't call a tribe of native Americans 'savages' or any other such name."

"Then, tell me, what *would* you call people who terrorize mine workers and steal private property? Just this morning I had a report of missing supplies. And the evidence points to those Indians."

"I don't know about that, but the number of Indians in this area is dwindling at a rate far in excess of anything we've ever seen before."

"From liquor and disease no doubt!" Claiborne said contemptuously, spouting an old and often incorrect cliche about how Indians in general lived their lives. "It's something they've brought on themselves."

"I see a cabinet in this office that contains more liquor than most of them will consume in a year," Mr. Bartlett shot back. "You've spent enough money on that stuff to keep at least one Indian family of six in food for many months!"

"But I have the money, Andy, and I shall spend it as I please. What *they* buy are the cheap turbo wines and beer that has gone flat. They don't care what year a wine originated so long as it allows them to get drunk, the sooner the better."

"Have *you* ever been drunk, Bob?"

"Not a relevant question!"

"Oh, it's relevant when you tell the big lie that Indians rot their guts out on cheap booze, but *not* relevant when you proclaim that you are doing it for a hundred dollars a bottle?"

The other man shot to his feet.

"You are indeed wearing out my patience," Claiborne said, his voice barely below the point of yelling.

Andrew Bartlett, now also standing, said, "Bob you head the largest mining company in the entire state. You have staked out a huge amount of land. Other tribes who live close to similar mines owned by your competitors aren't having nearly the problems this tribe is having. Do you have any idea what could be making such a difference?"

"Get out! Now!" Claiborne ordered as he angrily pressed a button on the side of his desk. "I won't sit here and listen to you blame me and my company for the deaths of those Indians."

"It's not that easy," Mr. Bartlett said calmly.

"Want to bet?"

The door to the office opened and two very large men entered.

"Escort this gentleman out of the building!" Claiborne ordered. "He is not to be allowed re-entry, ever!"

"I would suggest that you not do that," Mr. Bartlett said, in a cold tone well rehearsed over the years, as the result of practice in a variety of confrontations not unlike the one presently unfolding.

The two men glanced at Claiborne.

"Follow your orders!" he shouted.

Mr. Bartlett instantly whipped out a compact mobile phone from the inside pocket of his business suit.

"This is Andrew Bartlett," he spoke into the tiny microphone, after pressing a single number on the dialing pad. "I'm here for the Skull Junction assignment. Please tell FBI Director Sessions that the nearest unit in the western sector may be needed shortly. If you don't hear from me within the next two hours, this is code red. Check with the Oval Office if you need corroboration."

He slipped the phone back into his pocket.

As he folded his arms in front of him, Andrew Bartlett looked from one man to the other, and said, calmly, "Your move, gentlemen!"

 **Five**

Chad had managed to get the motorcycle started again, but the fuel gauge registered almost empty. So he and Ryan followed Brook-That-Sings and the other braves back to their village a few miles from the spot where the jeep had wrecked.

To call where the tribe lived a village seemed an exaggeration. What the brothers saw was actually nothing more than a few adobe huts and a couple of tepees and, acting as a backdrop, a water tower.

"It leads in to the well that used to serve this tribe for more than a century without difficulty," Brook-That-Sings told them.

"But no longer?" Ryan asked.

"Yes, Ryan, we still drink from it, but all of us suspect that it is the source of our troubles," their new friend told them. "Yet, what are we supposed to do? Die of thirst instead?"

They were introduced to Brook-That-Sings' wife, a beautiful young woman called Warm Sun.

"Beautiful names," Chad said.

"Logical also," Brook-That-Sings told him, "if you realize all the details of the way we live. Let me show you what I mean."

Brook-That-Sings approached one hut, then another, and a third. Soon four other Indians had joined him.

"This is Sweet Flower," he said, introducing a pretty teenage girl who couldn't take her eyes off Chad.

Brook-That-Sings turned to the second one, a large man who was in his mid-forties.

"This is Tall Timber," Brook-That-Sings added.

The next Indian was a woman who was so slight, so fragile that it seemed the slightest breeze would carry her away.

"My wife's sister is named Morning Mist," he said proudly.

And then he came to the fourth member of that small group.

This one was a young man, about twenty-five years of age, and obviously suffering from severe retardation.

"Lost Dreams," Brook-That-Sings told them.

Ryan approached Lost Dreams, saw someone with a large, strong-looking frame who would never be other than a child in his mind.

"Lost Dreams couldn't have been affected by the water," Ryan pointed out. "This happened many years ago."

"You are correct, Ryan," Brook-That-Sings replied. "But he still stands as a monument to what white men in safe offices thousands of miles away have decreed for my people."

"Explain," Chad asked.

"Lost Dreams wasn't given proper medical care. Qualified doctors just weren't available out here twenty-three years ago. By the time his parents could reach the nearest hospital, the high fever had already done its damage and caused my friend to be what you see now."

Ryan turned away from Lost Dreams.

"Chad, we need to get back to town and tell Dad about the problems here. Something needs to be done quickly before these people have more tragedy in their lives."

"Ryan, we don't have enough fuel to get back to town, unless there's some here in the village we can buy."

"I'm afraid not," said Brook-That-Sings. "Our supplies won't be here until tomorrow morning, and all the vehicles we have in the village have gone to town to help bring back supplies."

"Do you have a phone?" asked Chad, thinking they could at least let their dad know where they were.

"We do, but the line to the only phone in the village was mysteriously cut yesterday. So, my friends, tonight you will be our honored guests," said Brook-That-Sings. "Then tomorrow after the supply truck arrives, you can go into town."

Ryan and Chad nodded, knowing that their father would be alarmed when they did not return that evening, but not knowing what else to do.

"Good!" Brook-That-Sings replied. "You'll see that, though we live in a primitive manner, we know how to be hospitable."

# Six

Two hours later, the two brothers indeed had been treated with courtesy and simple human warmth.

"This is really delicious, Warm Sun," Ryan said as he sat in one of the huts, scooping up in a wooden ladle something that looked like stew from an earthen bowl.

Chad nodded agreement, eagerly consuming the thick mixture from the bowl he held.

"Crunchy," he said, rolling his eyes from side to side.

"We have so little red meat here," Brook-That-Sings told them. "We have to find substitutes."

"This isn't meat?" Chad said, genuinely surprised, because he had assumed that it was just that.

"You're kidding," Ryan added. "It has the texture of meat."

"Yes, part of the stew does."

Ryan and Chad glanced at one another.

Brook-That-Sings saw this and started laughing.

"You probably think it's earthworms and caterpillars, things like that," he said, chuckling.

They both breathed a sigh of relief.

"We really did," Chad admitted.

"Good," Brook-That-Sings added. "You're right. But don't worry . . . they're fresh. And the cooking process kills all the germs!"

All of a sudden, the two brothers needed some fresh air.

The campfire felt good as an evening chill enveloped the village. Just about everyone who lived there was seated around its reassuring flames.

"Sorry about the food," Brook-That-Sings said, a slight smile remaining. "We are so accustomed to the old ways."

"We have many restrictions on hunting," Tall Timber told them. "And we can scarcely afford even the cheaper cuts of beef. So, we have to fall back on what remains from the way our ancestors managed to fill their stomachs."

"Try this," said Sweet Dreams who happened to be sitting next to Chad.

"Thanks . . ." he replied, a little hesitant after the earlier "meal."

"Wild berries in goat's milk," she said, giggling.

Chad glanced at this new bowl with some apprehension, then took the wooden ladle Sweet Dreams handed to him, and dipped out some of the white-and-red concoction.

"Delicious!" he said almost instantly.

Ryan eagerly reached for the bowl and did the same.

"You're right," he beamed. "Just great!"

After the pleasant talk, and the little tidbits of berries and milk, the conversation became sad again.

"How did you come by your name?" Ryan asked, with real interest, of Brook-That-Sings.

Quite solemnly, their new friend threw his head back, glancing at the clear sky and the vast number of stars visible that evening.

"My mother, Bright Dawn, who has gone to be with the Lord now, gave it to me. One morning when I was a tiny baby, she carried me on her back to a stream in the mountains. As she sat by its side, watching the clear, beautiful waters, I stopped fretting, clearly enjoying the happy sound of the rushing water."

Ryan's eyes widened in recognition.

"We've been to places like that," he said, remembering some moments wistfully. "Our mother was still alive then, and she went along with us most of the time. She liked listening to the sound of the water rushing over the rocks. She thought it sounded a little like music."

Brook-That-Sings was smiling with appreciation.

"Sweet memories are wonderful," he said.

Then his expression changed.

"Until we realize that they are just that, until we say good-bye to someone who was part of them."

"How did your mother die?" Ryan asked.

"The same way so many others here die—the lack of proper health care," Brook-That-Sings said. "Then my father couldn't endure life without her. So he walked off into the mountains. A blizzard kicked up. We found his body days later."

At bed time that evening, Ryan and Chad followed Brook-That-Sings to an empty hut.

"There are blankets inside," the Indian told them. "I hope you sleep well, my friends."

"Where does Lost Dreams sleep?" Chad asked.

"In my hut. But it is not easy to have him with my wife and me."

"No privacy . . ." Chad said knowingly.

"More than that. This innocent one has terrible dreams, Chad Bartlett. These make him wake up screaming. Or else Lost Dreams walks outside, and I have to go after him. There are rattlesnakes all over this region. We used to have to worry only about them and the lizards, the gila monsters. But, now, so much more concerns me, so much more that is just as deadly."

Brook-That-Sings shook hands with both of them, then left for his own hut.

The interior of the boys' hut seemed grim, with only strange Indian masks on the walls, one of them with a white-feathered headdress around it. An odor of ancient earth hung so heavily in the air that it made them both cough at first, until they somehow were able to get used to it.

"Oh, Chad, we *have* to get to Dad as soon as possible!" Ryan exclaimed. "I know he's worried about us. And these people can't be allowed to suffer any more than they have. Living like this is bad enough, but dying like they have been doing. . . . Dad has to have the facts, has to be able to do something to help them."

"I agree," his brother replied. "In the morning, we'll get some fuel and head back to town."

"If somebody else doesn't intercept us again," added Ryan, his voice trembling a bit.

 **Seven**

Robert Claiborne had come to believe that he wasn't capable of feeling much, if any, guilt, because the quest for profits for his company, ClaStar Oil and Silver, had long ago replaced conscience.

And yet, having read some disturbing facts, Claiborne began to wonder if even he could find guilt nibbling at the corners of a mind that usually thought of guilt as a particularly irksome weakness.

"So, it's true then . . ." he said out loud, though there was no one else in his office at that moment. "That tribe has been suffering disease at a rate much higher than anyone has told me. People have been dying because . . . because—." He tried to brush that possibility out of his mind, but it wouldn't go, lingering there like confetti on wet cement.

That's what Bartlett was telling me. He tried to point out to me just how serious the situation had become, Claiborne thought sadly. *But I went and pulled my power act on him and tried to intimidate one of the most influential men in Washington, D.C.!*

He crumpled up the sheet of computer paper and threw it into a trash basket next to his desk.

When I checked over the past few months, everyone told me that things were fine.

He frowned deeply.

Why would they lie? Who could be responsible for this?

Claiborne stood, and walked over to the double-sized picture window that took up almost one entire wall in his office.

So very beautiful, he sighed.

He enjoyed for the thousandth time the clearest possible view of a series of mountain peaks at the horizon, each capped by snow, all of them majestic under a cloudless sky.

Claiborne opened the window, taking the clear air into his eager lungs, enjoying the feel of it throughout his body.

I got the adjoining land honestly, he told himself. *And I don't see any reason why our mining operation should be a health hazard to the Indians on the reservation. I've always insisted that my companies operate within the environmental codes.*

Claiborne turned back toward his desk, and recalled the emotional confrontation with Andrew Bartlett just an hour earlier.

He acted as though the wrath of God would descend upon me at any moment. How dare he come in here and treat me in that manner?

Just then the phone rang.

He picked up the neon-colored receiver.

"Bardens and Samuels are dead, sir," the voice told him. "We found their bodies an hour ago on the reservation. And Chutney is missing."

"How did Bardens and Samuels die?" Claiborne asked. "And what were they doing on the reservation? They were supposed to be patroling company property boundaries."

"Their jeep overturned, Mr. Claiborne. Both of them were crushed to death almost instantly."

"An accident?"

"I don't think so, sir."

"Why do you say that?"

"Arrows . . ."

"Arrows?"

"We uncovered a number of arrows at the site. It was one of these that had punctured a tire."

"You're saying they were attacked? It sounds like something out of an old cowboys-and-Indians movie."

"I don't know what else to make of it, sir."

"Keep looking for Chutney. Update me regularly."

"Will do."

The connection was broken.

Curling his hands into fists, Robert Claiborne mentally brushed aside even the smallest amount of guilt he may have been feeling.

Anger had replaced it.

# Eight

Ryan had been dreaming of a huge herd of buffalo, the sound of their pounding the ground like a storm that had been unleashed. All that was missing was the lightning and the rain.

Chad dreamed, too, but unlike Ryan, he fancied himself a strong warrior, hunting game in a forest, his muscular body honed by outdoor life, and not the weight-training equipment with which he usually worked.

"Ryan? Chad?"

A voice woke them up.

It was Brook-That-Sings, standing in the doorway of their tepee, moonlight outlining his form.

Ryan glanced at his watch.

Past midnight.

"What's wrong, friend?" Chad said, worried that something else had happened.

"I . . . I . . . well . . . there is something I've not told you," Brook-That-Sings replied, though unable to look at them directly.

"What's that?" Chad asked.

"We have a prisoner."

That one woke up the two brothers like a bucket of cold water thrown across their faces.

"I mean, he *was* a prisoner of sorts until a short while ago," Brook-That-Sings continued. "I didn't want either of you to know anything about him until I was certain that he was who he claimed to be."

"Certain of him about what?" Ryan asked.

"That he was genuine, that he wasn't just humoring us while he looked for a chance to escape. I wanted you to be aware of the fact that he has given us a horrible truth."

"Escape? Truth?" remarked Chad, genuinely puzzled. "Brook-That-Sings, I've got to tell you that you're not making much sense."

"I know. I know. What has been happening is terrible for my people and me, in ways you could never imagine, Chad. Please, come with me. The man I mentioned can explain better than I."

The man did just that.

Ryan and Chad sat in front of David Chutney, who was in his early twenties. He looked as though he had just come from a surfing contest

40

either at Malibu Beach or Hawaii's famed North Shore—tall, well-muscled, his blond hair long, a strand of it dangling down over his forehead.

"You were hired by ClaStar Oil and Silver to measure and then continue monitoring the water and soil pollution level in this area?" Ryan asked.

"That sounds pretty conscientious, doesn't it?"

"That's what they told me at the beginning," Chutney replied. "And it might actually have started out that way."

"Who's 'they'?" Chad probed.

"Two men who work for the founder-owner of ClaStar, Robert Claiborne."

"And you found out that the pollutant level was dangerously high?" asked Ryan this time.

"I did, and I told these guys about it. They sent me in with a load of chemicals that was supposed to help clean it up."

"What's wrong with that?" Ryan went on.

"To be honest, that's what *I* thought for a while," Chutney agreed. "None of the containers was marked or identified in any way. There was absolutely no reason to be suspicious."

"When did you become concerned?" Chad took up the questioning.

"I had some time off, so I decided, I guess it was a few weeks later, to do a little testing on my own. I discovered that the level of pollution was substantially worse instead of better."

"Because the chemicals were *making* it worse!" Ryan exclaimed. "It wasn't negligence, since they were doing more than ignoring what was wrong. They deliberately poisoned—."

Ryan's face was red as he took off his glasses, and began twirling them around by one earpiece as he tried to calm himself down.

"You got it right," Chutney told him. "I decided to play ignorant at first, then, later, I confessed my suspicions but in a way that told them I couldn't care less. I just didn't want to be deceived."

"What did they say then?" Chad asked, both fascinated and repelled at the same time.

Chutney bit his lower lip, hesitant, knowing that he was in a situation that was more than a little treacherous. He was putting his life on the line as a result of what he had been revealing to strangers. He was not afraid of the Indians. But he did fear the men who were responsible for this deadly plot to destroy innocent men, women, *and* children.

"Those guys thought I was one of them at that point. So, they confided in me that a vein of rich silver ore had been traced to the reservation here. And they offered me a percentage if I was willing to work with them. I thought if I pretended to play along with them, I'd have a chance to get some solid evidence against them."

Brook-That-Sings jumped to his feet and tried to walk off a sudden, understandable burst of anger.

"Isn't that something?" he said, his voice trembling. "We live in near-poverty, and yet, wealth lies below our feet!"

Chutney became nearly as emotional.

"I promise," he said. "I had no knowledge until recently of what was going on."

"They had no clue that you felt as you did?" Chad asked.

"I don't think so."

"Were the guys in the jeep, the men who hired you?" Ryan added

"No, from the way Brook-That-Sings described them, they were guards at the mine who were also in on the plot."

"Did you use the walkie-talkie we found to tell them that you were in trouble?"

"No!" Chutney protested. "I would rather be with Brook-That-Sings and his people than those guys anytime."

"But I thought you were playing along," Ryan persisted.

"That's right, but I still didn't signal—!" His eyes widened as he made the connection.

"They were going to *kill* me," he said. "They knew where I was, but Brook-That-Sings got to me first."

"Sounds about right," Ryan suggested, remembering the loud, harsh voice and the message they had intercepted on the walkie-talkie just before the jeep took out after them.

Hey, where have you been? . . . You haven't run into any of the tribe, have you? You're not letting those savages scare you off? In a few months we won't have to worry at all. They'll be dead, the entire tribe. You know that as well as I. Do what you're supposed to and get the devil back here!

Ryan quickly told David Chutney what Chad and he had heard earlier that day.

"That must have been directed at the men in the jeep who were sent to *kill* me!" Chutney blurted out.

"We thought they were after the two of us," Ryan said. "But they weren't, at least not at first, anyway. If Brook-That-Sings hadn't gotten to you, you probably wouldn't be alive now, David."

Chutney's face was drained of all color, and he felt dizzy.

"How could I have gotten into this awful business?" he asked of himself and those who were with him. "I never thought I could be so blind, so stupid. I care very much about what is happening to Native Americans. That's why I accepted the job in the first place."

"And as far as you knew, you went to work for a supposedly honorable company," Chad pointed out, feeling some of the young man's personal anguish. "When you learned what was being done to these people, you decided to help by digging out evidence that would stop them dead. I don't think you've been doing *anything* that was wrong."

"You're right about the evidence, Chad. I've got lots of records, including dates, other test results, more stuff than you could imagine."

He reached into one pocket of his light blue jeans.

"Here it is," he said as he held up the little film canister. "I think we can hang them with this."

As he put the film back into his pocket, he added, "I'm not sure that Claiborne himself is aware of what's going on."

"How could that be?" asked Brook-That-Sings. "He founded the company. He owns it. It bears part of his name."

"Greedy men can be very good at creating a lot of deception," Chutney remarked. "It's been done before—in the Federal government, in the banking industry, and elsewhere."

"But what, really, could *they* get out of it?" Ryan asked.

"The better the company's profits, the more money those guys earn through their stock options and bonuses. And if they find a way to acquire that valuable silver vein, then promotions can be added to the list."

"I know more than ever that Dad can help," Ryan told them earnestly. "This involves certain illegal Federal as well as state activities. All Dad has to do is pick up a phone and call the Federal Trade Commission, the Department of Energy, and the FBI!"

"And the Justice Department," Chad added to the list. "We can bring them down *if* you're willing to be a witness."

"Your dad's got me for as long as I'm needed."

"Praise God!" Ryan said almost at a shout.

 **Nine**

The *next morning* . . .

Nick Moore and Sam Barbour thought that everything was going their way. Robert Claiborne believed that two security guards and David Chutney had been killed by the Indians on the nearby reservation.

"He never asked why those Indians would have killed them," Barbour remarked as they sat in an office at the ClaStar Oil and Silver building.

"Of couse not. It was only natural for Claiborne to blame the Indians after all that stuff we'd been feeding him about Indians terrorizing workers at the mine," Moore told him. "Claiborne may be aggressive and all that, but the death of anyone, especially three of his employees, is guaranteed to make him act crazy. He always comes down strong against what he thinks is wrong."

Moore and Barbour made an odd combination from a physical standpoint. Moore was only a little over five feet tall and had a very dark complexion, while Barbour was six-feet-five inches tall, and had pale pinkish skin. But the two men were absolutely identical when it came to their ruthless outlook.

"What do we do about this Bartlett character?" Moore asked. "I say we make sure he's not around much longer."

Barbour sat up straight in his chair and stared at the other man.

"That would be a mistake," he said. "How come you can't see that right away, Nick?"

"Maybe I'm just stupid, old buddy. I guess I need to have you explain everything to me in one-syllable words."

"Anybody who is National Security Advisor is *not* a character, but somebody who could destroy this scheme of ours with just a few phone calls and send us off to federal prison."

"But there's no proof," Moore reminded him. "And government sting operations are out of favor these days. What in the world do you think either of us have to worry about?"

"This!" Barbour pointed abruptly to a portable black tape recorder on top of his desk.

"So what's that supposed to mean?" Moore asked.

"Listen! It was recorded just a few minutes ago. Our man hurried it over to me right away."

Barbour turned on the recorder.

Voice One: I have serious concerns here, My boys are missing. I've contacted the local authorities. Ryan and Chad didn't come back from a motorcycle ride into the desert yesterday. Somehow I think their disappearance could be linked to the Indian health problem. There was also a jeep accident that killed two ClaStar employees yesterday.

Voice Two: What do you suspect?

Voice One: That someone or a group of individuals is conspiring to wipe out an entire tribe of Native Americans.

Voice Two: That sounds like Hitler during World War II.

Voice One: It's cut from a similar cloth, Mr. President.

Moore interrupted, "Sam, is that Bartlett and the—?"

Barbour shut him up with a cold, cruel expression.

The tape recording continued:

Voice Two: What help do you need, Andrew?

Voice One: Availability of the National Guard at a moment's notice.

Voice Two: You've got that. Use Code Red. Is there anything else I can do, my friend?

Voice One: Firearms for myself.

Voice Two: No problem, Andrew. I'll send someone from the FBI regional office. He'll be sure

*and bring a supply along with him. But, let me
ask this: Why for yourself?*

*Voice One: Ryan and Chad have been gone all
night, Mr. President. I may have to do something
at a moment's notice. Right now the sheriff has
asked me to stay close to the phone, in case the
boys try to call.*

*Voice Two: I understand that, Andrew. I'll have
Director Sessions call Art Simpson as soon as I
hang up. The two of you have met. Is Simpson all
right with you?*

Voice One: Good man. Good choice, Mr. President.

*Voice Two: He'll be at Skull Junction in about
two hours. I think Route 53 would be a good, less
obvious way to go, don't you?*

*Voice One: Exactly right, Mr. President. That is
the choice I myself would have made.*

Voice Two: Bless you, Andrew . . .

Voice One: I am indebted to you, Mr. President.

Voice Two: My prayers go with you.

Voice One: Thank you, Mr. President.

Nick Moore and Sam Barbour glanced at one
another.

"It's a good thing we *own* the manager of that
hotel and most of the staff," Moore said.

"Now you see how terrible all of this is!" Barbour
exclaimed. "It's gotten far beyond anything we
imagined."

"Then it only means one thing—that we've got to keep that FBI agent Simpson from ever getting as far as Skull Junction and Bartlett."

"You *are* crazy, Nick."

Moore folded his arms across his chest and said, "All right, then, what's the alternative?"

Barbour had no answer.

"It's decided, okay? He'll have an unfortunate 'accident,' and we'll blame it on the tribe," Moore said triumphantly.

His partner's eyes widened at that notion.

"And then we must find those kids and get rid of them as well!" he added. "With the right 'evidence,' we can make those redskins the villains again, and have them blamed for all three deaths. Because of his tragic loss, Bartlett will be turned against a bunch of savages rather than us!"

"Bullseye!" Moore replied gleefully. "It'll be just like in the old West!"

Ten

Ryan and Chad had filled the motorcycle with fuel and were ready to leave the village. David Chutney and Brook-That-Sings walked up to them.

"I don't know what to say to any of you," Chutney said, looking from the Bartletts to the Indian. "I feel so ashamed that all this has happened, and that I was a part of it for a while."

"But, now, you belong to the solution," Chad pointed out.

"Where do you go now?" Ryan asked.

"One of Brook-That-Sings' friends is taking me to a town a few miles from here. I'll stay with a buddy of mine from college days who lives there. If any of the Feds want to see me, this is where I'll be for a few weeks or until my money runs out, anyway."

He thanked the three of them, and then walked

back toward one of the Native Americans who was waving to him.

Brook-That-Sings reached out his hand, and first Ryan, then Chad shook it.

"I hope you get to your father soon, and that he listens," the Indian said. "We need to do something, or we all will die, either by what they are doing to our water and soil, or because my people will strike back in revenge."

He saw how startled they were by that statement.

"We are Christians now, yes," Brook-That-Sings went on, "but it is hard not to strike back at those who wound us, at those who rob from us the lives of our loved ones. I admit, it has been that way for generations, blood for blood. Being followers of the Prince of Peace helps restrain those impulses, but they are still there, my friends. And it is a battle to keep them under control, to continue honoring our Savior when our very lives are being threatened."

"Dad is the one you need to get on your side," Ryan assured him. "I don't think he'll be hard to convince. After all, what you are experiencing is the reason he's here in the first place!"

"You might be in some danger," Brook-That-Sings remarked. "They've attacked you before."

"That's true," Ryan agreed. "Why don't you fol—?"

"We've been planning on that whether you asked or not," Brook-That-Sings said, smiling broadly. "We *have* learned some useful things from our warriors of the past—this is one of those, Ryan my friend. You will never know we're nearby. And *they* won't either."

"Thank you for your friendship," Chad said.

"It's new, but it's in the Lord," Brook-That-Sings added, "and that means it *will* endure."

They couldn't take the chance of doing the job themselves, so Nick Moore and Sam Barbour pulled someone from another department, a big guy named Bruno Heathly who had done some crucial dirty work before.

"Can you handle it?" Nick Moore asked.

"This'll be easy," Heathly assured him.

"Good!" Moore said, patting him on the back. "You've been taking chances over the past couple of years, Bruno. Once we get the Indians' land, I can promise you rewards like you wouldn't believe! Much more than the money you're getting today."

"Our deal is working out just fine already," Heathly beamed. "That projection TV is just great. And those old bills of mine are gone! I have no debt now. Anything else would be terrific."

"Like an executive position with this company?" Barbour said, dangling the enticement.

"Anything you decide is fine with me," Heathly replied, though with an odd tone to his voice.

He started to leave the office, then he turned and seemed about to say something.

"What can we do for you, Bruno?" Barbour asked.

"Nothing," he said, with a bit of awkwardness and hesitancy that was quite uncustomary, for they had never met a man more aggressive and determined than Bruno Heathly.

After he had left, Moore and Barbour looked at one another, trying not to be concerned.

Bruno Heathly had stopped at a rocky lookout point just short of two miles from Skull Junction.

Directly ahead and below stretched narrow, ill-kept Route 53. And a single automobile coming closer.

But Heathly was even more hesitant than he had let on back at the office. For he could hardly admit to *himself* what he had not been able to tell Nick Moore and Sam Barbour.

Nightmares.

Ever since he had learned what was happening to the Indians in that village, Heathly had been having nightmares, usually involving sick women and children. He saw their faces torn by pain, their bodies pale, thin skin stretched tightly over bones.

I've tried so hard not to let any of that get to me, he thought. *For a while there, it worked. I could sleep straight through the night.*

Tears rolled down his cheeks.

But it's started again. In my dreams, I see dying children stumbling toward me, accusing me of being their murderer.

He glanced at his watch.

That FBI guy Simpson should be passing by soon. I'm supposed to kill him. I'm supposed to take a rifle, and point it at him, and kill him dead, then plant the rifle in one of the tepees just as those Indians are confronted by the authorities, including this Bartlett.

The man's children.

Heathly was also assigned the job of eliminating both of *them,* so that Andrew Bartlett himself, motivated by such devastating personal tragedy, would turn against the tribe.

As for whomever the murders could be directly pinned on, the death penalty seemed likely.

And I'm in the midst of it all, Heathly told himself. *I'm the guy picked to murder three more human beings.*

Three more . . . in addition to the dozen or so others who would most likely die in the weeks and months to come, after slowly being poisoned by contaminated water.

Bruno Heathly dropped the rifle and brought his hands to his forehead, letting out a scream that carried far further than he ever intended.

# Eleven

Short, thin, middle-aged but in top-notch physical shape, reflexes well-honed, Arthur Simpson, veteran special agent for the Federal Bureau of Investigation, heard the scream.

His air conditioner wasn't working; the car windows were open. The screaming was propelled by a special anguish in the very sound.

Simpson slammed on the car brakes, the vehicle groaning from the sudden halt.

In an instant he had opened the door and slid out, belly-down on the pock-marked road.

Simpson held a Smith and Wesson revolver in his left hand and dragged himself along with his right hand.

Slowly he raised himself up to the level of the trunk lid.

North.

He heard the sound coming from a northerly direction.

Bureau training made each agent much like a super-cop, taking the skills of local police officers and adding to these. Instantly detecting the source of any such screaming was part of what he had picked up, both from training and from many years of experience with terrorists, bank robbers and others.

The mountains were half a mile north.

Closer was a tall pile of rocks. Otherwise Simpson saw only flat desert, with no obvious life.

A tall pile of rocks.

It had to have come from there. The mountains were too far away for the sound to have carried as far as that.

Only silence now.

Only—.

No!

Another sound.

He strained to hear it, since it was lower, less distinct than the first.

Sobbing.

Someone was sobbing.

Knowing it could be a trick, a ploy to get him to show himself more fully, Simpson hesitated.

But only for a moment.

There was a special urgency to the sound.

Simpson bent nearly in half as he left the shelter of the car and hurried across an open portion of sand, to the base of the rocks, which had been piled thirty-some-odd feet high.

As he was getting ready to climb up, an all-too-familiar sound ripped through the air.

A rifle being fired.

Closeby. . . .

He flattened himself as much as possible against the rocks.

No more.

That was the first shot . . . the only one.

A minute or two later, he saw the rifle being thrown over the edge. It landed not far from his feet.

Again, Simpson knew, this could be a not-so-clever trick. Whoever it was might have other weapons.

He was sweating.

The morning chill was being replaced by an increasing desert heat.

That was when he heard the motorcycle.

Even before Simpson saw it, he wondered if it could be the missing Bartlett brothers. He had been told they were traveling on some kind of fancy off-road bike.

His mind went back years before, to the days when he was tempted to buy a big motorcycle and just set off across the country.

How I loved that baby! he thought. *How I loved the idea of the open road, the wind across my face,*

*the sun overhead, the power of that motorcycle tak-
ing me wherever I wanted to go.*

He sighed, with a touch of regret.

*That was one of my fantasies when I was
younger. The other was to become an FBI agent,
what they used to call a G-man. Well, at least, it
turned out that one of my dreams did come true.*

He saw the approaching motorcycle now, two
teenagers seated on it, its impressive bulk speed-
ing across the desert, not far from the pile of rocks.

Be careful, the President of the United States
had said during an unusual phone call that came
directly from the Oval Office, with FBI Director
Sessions also on the line. *Andy Bartlett's sons may
be in danger, Arthur. This is a special assignment,
please be aware of that. . . .*

Simpson knew he had to do something immediately, knew he had to storm the lookout spot
where the screams and sobbing had originated,
and from which the rifle had been tossed.

*Or dropped quite accidentally, in a careless
moment!* the man exclaimed to himself.

Holding his breath, his muscles tensed, he saw
a flatter section of rocks that he could inch along,
toward the top. This he did, and jumped up, holding his revolver straight out in front of him, aimed,
as it turned out, at a man who was curled up into
a round shape, sobbing like a baby.

Standing next to him was an Indian.

"My name is Brook-That-Sings," the handsome young man said. "You don't have to worry. He's not interested in hurting anyone now."

"How did you get up the other side?" Simpson asked, astonished. "I didn't hear anything."

Brook-That-Sings smiled.

"My people have ways," he said, enjoying the moment. "Centuries of living out in the open have taught us much."

 # Twelve

Bruno Heathly confessed everything. Brook-That-Sings was ready to grab the man and kill him on the spot.

No, Lord, he thought, fighting the urge that rose up so strongly inside him. *I won't do that. Even though a part of me wants to get my hands around his neck and take immediate revenge, my soul won't allow me to do so. And nothing I could do, now, would bring back any of those who died because of him and the men who sent him.*

The Bartlett brothers had stopped to see what was going on at the rock pile.

"I honestly didn't think it was going to be so bad for those Indians," Bruno sobbed as they gathered at the base of that rock pile. "At first I thought they'd just get sick."

"Oh, just a little upset stomach, that sort of thing?" Arthur Simpson asked sarcastically.

"Yes, *yes!*" Heathly responded. "I thought what

we were doing was going to do nothing more than that. It's part of the plan, those guys told me. There would be just a little sickness, a little disease, that's all, a self-contained epidemic of sorts, but nobody would die. *'They'll be just uncomfortable; women and babies won't die!'* That's what they said. . . . And eventually the tribe would have to be relocated to a non-polluted area. . . . "

"And the land put up for sale?" asked Brook-That-Sings.

His head bowed, Heathly nodded.

"Then ClaStar could move in, buy the land at bargain prices and earn billions from all that silver!" Ryan exclaimed.

"And you cooperated because this was *all* that was supposed to happen?" remarked Brook-That-Sings. "An entire tribe forced to leave their homes and start over someplace else. Their health ruined!"

"Who are the men responsible?" Simpson asked. "I assume it was from the top down—Robert Claiborne and others."

"No, no," Heathly answered. "It all was supposed to be kept from him. Claiborne would never have approved."

"He never realized what was happening?"

"Not even a hint, until a couple of days ago. Even now, he doesn't realize *everything!*"

Simpson pulled out a palm-sized mobile phone from an inside pocket of the jacket he was wearing.

"I'm going to call Andrew Bartlett," he said. "He's got to know what's happening. Then we'll all wait here for the local authorities."

Andrew Bartlett heard only that his sons were safe; then some kind of interference broke the mobile connection. Moments later the phone rang again, but this time it wasn't Simpson. . . .

 # Thirteen

Minutes later Mr. Bartlett was sitting in the same soft-leather chair in the same plush office at ClaStar Oil and Silver as on the day before. But in no way was he talking to anyone who seemed like the same man.

Robert Claiborne had changed . . . dramatically.

Yesterday he had been angry at what Andrew Bartlett had told him. But what he learned since then had shaken him to his very gut.

"I don't know what to say," he told Mr. Bartlett. "It's only been twenty-four hours, but I feel as though a lifetime has passed. Just a short while ago, I was ready to command an army of bulldozers and level that Indian village to the ground. I thought the tribe was responsible for the deaths of three of my employees."

"You knew nothing?" Mr. Bartlett asked, his voice full of doubt. "That does seem a little bizarre."

"Not a clue."

"How could that be?"

"You hire men with only one motive: making money for you. And you give them complete freedom because you trust their instincts," Claiborne explained.

. . . making money for you.

Mr. Bartlett had seen the impact of greed upon countless numbers of innocent people around the world. In some countries, it meant that the rulers became immensely wealthy while the ordinary citizens wallowed in conditions that included open sewers, polluted water, rag-clothed children with dirty faces bumming money from tourists.

"I have never been hungry," Claiborne was saying. "I have never been without clothes, without heat, without a new car. Poverty was something the thought of which filled me with terror, because it meant the crumbling of my entire world, *everything* being taken away from me.

"So, I became determined that I would *always* have money. And I did anything necessary to ensure that—."

"—no matter how illegal or unethical—!"

"You are very wrong!" Claiborne yelled, his face red, his breath coming in rapid spurts. "I always assumed the people around me would be as honest as I have tried to be throughout my professional life."

"And how honest *are* you?" Mr. Bartlett demanded.

"If you only knew," the other man said, "if you only knew."

"Well, I *don't* know. Tell me!"

He didn't get the chance.

Nick Moore and Sam Barbour stormed into his office.

"What are you doing to us?" Moore demanded.

"I'm firing you both," Claiborne said.

"Why?" Barbour asked angrily.

"Because of this."

Claiborne reached into the center drawer of his desk and took out a file folder containing a thick pile of papers.

"All the evidence I need," he said coldly, tapping the folder, as he stared down the other man.

Barbour grabbed it, leafing through the contents, his face suddenly very pale, and then he passed the folder to Moore.

"How long did it take you to get all this stuff?" Moore asked, his face twisted into a sneer.

"The past twenty-four hours," replied Claiborne. "This company still has some honest individuals left on the payroll, people who don't confuse dedication with obsession over money."

The two men said nothing further but threw the file and its contents onto the floor and stalked out of the office.

"Dangerous men," Mr. Bartlett observed as he bent down and picked up the scattered sheets of paper and the folder itself.

"Not any more," Claiborne told him confidently. "Those contents will hang them."

Mr. Bartlett looked at some of the material.

"Memos from one to the other," he said. "Receipts for special poisons that they had had concocted for them. *Wait a minute!*"

Claiborne sighed as he said, "You must be looking at what produced a similar reaction from me."

"Someone in the Department of Indian Affairs was being paid off by them," Mr. Bartlett commented, with disgust in his voice. "I know the man, though I wish I didn't, frankly. The irony is that he's highly thought of. He goes around the country making speeches, trying to get people to help improve life for Native Americans. At the same time he's cooperating with a plot to murder dozens of them!"

"Should it surprise you?" Claiborne asked.

"Of course not—but it does."

Claiborne started trembling then, so much so that Mr. Bartlett thought he might be in the midst of some sort of seizure.

"Are you—?" he started to say.

Claiborne waved his hand impatiently.

"It's nothing, Mr. Bartlett," he said, "nothing physical as such. It's just that everything is flooding in on me now. You see. While it may have been the monstrous crimes of two of my men that created a nightmare for that tribe, it was *my* example that spurred them on."

"An example that, clearly, they misunderstood."

"But how much of that deadly error do I, Robert Claiborne, bear responsibility for? Doesn't your Bible say something about avoiding all appearance of the practice of evil?

"I didn't do that, you know. They saw me as a man possessed by the pursuit of more and more wealth. And they caught a hold of this and turned it into something even uglier."

He found himself unable to continue for several moments.

"I really don't have anyone, you see," Claiborne said finally, a dark expression on his face. "It's not easy getting used to life as I must live it, returning to an empty apartment on the third floor of this building, or one of my four homes in various parts of the world.

"My wife long ago divorced me. My son is confined to some institution for the insane, a drug addict crippled by his habit, with a shattered mind and body that the experts doubt they'll ever be able to piece together.

"This is my legacy. I'm seeing every bit of it before me right now, long before I die. And my heart feels as though someone has clasped a tight fist around it and won't let go.

"Whenever my loved ones turned to me, I had no time for them, showed them no warmth. I expressed my love through my checkbook. And now look at the latest results of the way I have lived and treated others."

He had been looking away. Now he turned, and his gaze met directly with Andrew Bartlett's own.

"Tell me, sir," he asked, pleading. "What is there left for me, realizing what I do now? Can you answer that? Can you?"

 # Fourteen

Nick Moore and Sam Barbour knew they were trapped. And they knew they could end up in jail for the rest of their lives.

"They might give us the death penalty!" Barbour said, his voice not much below a scream.

"You're right," Moore agreed. "But we're going to take a lot of people with us before that happens."

"What are you saying?"

"We're going to burn down this building and make sure the rest of the town goes up with it. And then we'll attack those savages and kill as many as we can!"

"I don't know about that, Nick," said Sam, realizing his partner's mind had snapped.

"You hate them as much as I do. You and I both had relatives with Custer, men slaughtered by Indians at Little Big Horn."

Barbour shrugged his shoulders, temporarily agreeing with his partner, but hoping Nick would soon come to his senses.

"In the basement," Moore added. "There's lots of flammable stuff. A couple of matches, and this whole building will go up."

Skull Junction buildings had been renovated over the years, but a deliberate attempt had been made to keep the "authentic" Western character intact. This was colorful and atmospheric, but it was also dangerous, since that meant the widespread use of wood as opposed to concrete and steel.

The ClaStar building, at the eastern end of town, had had to fit in with the others. This meant that, while only two years old, it *looked* as though it had been erected along with the rest of Skull Junction a century earlier.

"We can destroy everything," Moore said, his eyes wide, a wild expression on his face.

"But we still go to jail," Barbour protested. "And things will be much worse for us. We almost guarantee our execution."

"Don't doubt, for a second, that that's where we're *already* headed," Moore reminded him. "Let's cause the most commotion. Let's get the biggest headlines. The guy who rammed his car into that Texas cafeteria . . . look at the attention the media gave him!"

"But that psycho's dead now, and, you know, nobody remembers his name, Nick."

"Yet, for a few days, the whole country was aware of him. Doesn't that count for something?"

They shook hands, then, and headed for the basement of the three story building.

"Tell me, sir," Claiborne's plea still echoed in the room, *"What is there left for me, realizing what I do now? Can you answer that? Can you?"*

"I think you have the rest of your life left," Mr. Bartlett replied. "You're still the owner of ClaStar Oil and Silver. You have at least twenty very strong years remaining, perhaps more than that."

"To do what?" Claiborne asked. "To spend time by myself, no one caring about me, thinking endlessly about the suffering in that village, thinking about the pain I've caused those in my own family? If that's how the years will be spent, what *is* the point of living at all?"

. . . what is the point of living at all?

Mr. Bartlett could clearly hear in Robert Claiborne's voice and could easily see in the man's tormented expression that years of suppressed pain and buried guilt over past acts had jumped to the surface.

"Go to the people in that village and confess to them how you feel," Andrew Bartlett said finally.

"But they've suffered *such loss!* Surely, those people will only spit upon me, or worse. I could not blame them for that. I would do the same if I had endured what they have."

"*Let* one or two or a dozen show you their contempt in that manner or any other that occurs to them. Then stand tall, stand firm, stand in the peace of knowing that you are at last trying to make things right, as much as this can be done under the circumstances. Pour out your heart to them.

"They respond most to that which is the least artificial. These people have only contempt for hypocrisy. Give them what is *inside* you, without holding back, and they will give you themselves in return."

Robert Claiborne's eyes filled with tears.

"I wish it could be as you so eloquently indicate, I really do," he started to say . . . until a certain odor caught his attention, and he cocked his head, trying to discern where it was coming from.

Mr. Bartlett picked up on this instantly, and said, "Smoke . . . something's on fire."

"I wonder if those crazy—," Claiborne said, the possible truth hitting him as hard as any physical blow.

The two of them hurried out of the office and into the long corridor that adjoined it. Smoke alarms began to ring.

"Not the elevator," Bartlett shouted. "Where are the stairs?"

"This way," Claiborne motioned.

Chaos was already beginning among the employees and visitors in the building. People were rushing in sheer panic out of their offices, responding to the alarms and the combined odors of burning wood and fused electrical circuits and other materials.

"I think they intend to destroy everything," Claiborne added. "The company, Skull Junction, the tribe's village, *all of it!*"

Mr. Bartlett could not disagree with that. He wondered if his sons and he would ever see one another alive again.

# Fifteen

The fires could be seen from miles away, with smoke billowing up in black or gray clouds that made the scene in front of them seem like a typical day in Beirut, Lebanon, or war-torn Yugoslavia, not the American West!

The group at the desert rock pile had just finished filling in the Sheriff on everything that happened when they spotted the smoke.

"That fire is coming from Skull Junction," Ryan yelled.

Arthur Simpson turned to Bruno Heathly.

"The men you named," he said, "could they be the cause?"

Heathly nodded sadly.

"It is every bit what they are capable of," he replied. "What they can't have, they destroy."

Brook-That-Sings' shoulders slumped.

"Not again!" he exclaimed.

"What do you mean?" Simpson asked.

"Skull Junction got its name because it has always been a place of death . . . this whole area has!"

"What else has happened here?"

"A hundred years ago, a drunken cowboy set fire to the town, and every building was either burned to the ground or had to be demolished because of too much damage."

Brook-That-Sings was shuddering.

"But there's more: During the Civil War, several dozen slaves were kept here, out of reach of the Union Army. Their owners figured that the South would win the war, and the slaves could be returned to plantations in Georgia and elsewhere. But when the North won, all the slaves were murdered, their bodies buried somewhere in this area."

Tears dripped down his cheeks.

"And then there was what happened to *my* people," Brook-That-Sings told them, with special anguish. "Skull Junction was the scene of a massacre by cavalrymen. Soldiers took every man, every woman, every child and shot them to death. Their bodies, too, are buried somewhere around here. This is a place of great tragedy, great sorrow for so many!"

He flung his left arm in the direction of the increasing fire-and-smoke that was less than two miles away.

"And now this!" Brook-That-Sings said, sounding as though his heart was being torn from his body.

"I think all of us should head straight to Skull Junction," Arthur Simpson remarked, after a whispered word with the Sheriff, who had just received an urgent message on his car radio.

He turned toward Bruno Heathly.

"Will you help?" he asked warily. "It looks like we will need every able body to help fight this fire."

Heathly jumped to his feet.

"Yes, yes, I will!" he said.

"You realize, don't you, that whatever you do now to help will mean little or nothing in terms of getting you any special treatment for what you have caused over the past two years?"

"I know, I know. I'll still be sent to jail. But I can't stand by and do nothing this time, while others are dying."

Bruno Heathly didn't.

He didn't stand by while buildings burned, while people ran into the street, their clothes on fire.

He helped; he helped a great deal. He ran into the Sagebrush Inn, and carried out several elderly men and women who had been overcome by the heat and the smoke.

He did the same with anyone left inside the ClaStar building at the edge of town.

Including Andrew Bartlett and Robert Claiborne.

Both had gotten out well before the structure had been totally consumed. But they heard pathetic screams issuing from inside. Some employees hadn't been able to leave in time. So the two men had rushed back into the now-dangerous building to help them and became trapped!

Heathly got them both out, first dragging Claiborne to the street. Then he hurriedly went back for Mr. Bartlett, whose body was pinned under some heavy fallen crossbeams.

"Jesus, Jesus . . ." Mr. Bartlett was whispering.

"I *want* to believe, too," Heathly said. "But how can I ask Him to—?"

"He'll take . . . us anytime . . . during any . . . circumstance," Mr. Bartlett muttered, his strength nearly gone.

For a few seconds, Heathly bowed his head, crying as he, too, prayed.

Then he grabbed one of the two beams on top of Mr. Bartlett, straining under the weight he lifted it up and threw it to one side. As he was lifting the second beam, he felt a knife-splitting pain as muscle tissue inside his own body ripped. It caused him to stagger, but not before he disposed of the beam.

"We've got to get you out of here!" he declared, gritting his teeth as sharp, awful pain tore through his body.

"Man, you . . . can't . . . do . . . it!" Mr. Bartlett told him, weakly, his eyes half-shut "You're . . . badly . . . hurt."

Bruno Heathly ignored this. As he was lifting Andrew Bartlett, he noticed for a moment two lifeless bodies amidst the wreckage a few feet away.

Nick Moore and Sam Barbour.

Neither had survived. The results of their greed had collapsed on them, killing both instantly.

Heathly managed to get Mr. Bartlett to what was left of the front of the ClaStar building. Then he tripped on some glowing debris and fell.

Mr. Bartlett tried to grab him, but he was far too weak himself. Heathly was getting to his feet when a wall collapsed on him.

"*No!*" Mr. Bartlett screamed.

Moments later, Andrew Bartlett felt strong hands around his waist, as someone on the outside saw what had happened, rushed over, and pulled him out into the street, just as the rest of the structure caved in, accompanied by a loud sound much like the rolling clap of distant thunder.

 **Sixteen**

Scores of people had to be airlifted to the nearest hospital.

Fire departments were called in from a dozen communities within a seventy mile radius. By the time the flames had been brought under control and, then, put out altogether, nothing was left standing. All that remained of Skull Junction was blackened timbers and portions of walls and large piles of other debris.

At the nearest hospital, dozens of people were fighting for their lives.

Most made it, fully recovering their physical health as the weeks passed, but the damage done to their emotions would take much longer to heal.

Others did not leave the hospital alive and the bodies of some were flown back to hometowns elsewhere in the United States for burial.

Some of the survivors faced operation after operation long after pulling out of immediate danger; of these, more than half would carry the scars with them the rest of their lives.

For quite a number, coming back from the brink of death proved to be a process little short of miraculous.

That was how it was for Andrew Bartlett and Robert Claiborne.

Through their shared ordeal, the two men became exceptionally close friends. After they could be moved into wheelchairs, they spent hours together, in the corridors of the hospital or outside, taking in the clear air and glad to be alive.

"I thought there was just one advantage of having a great deal of money," Claiborne said. "I could buy *anything* with it—anything I ever needed or wanted. Since I had been healthy all my life, what we have experienced and seen here was farthest from my mind."

What we have experienced and seen here . . .

Claiborne arranged to have a team of international burn specialists flown in from half a dozen countries in addition to those he gathered from the United States, not only to treat himself, but to take care of Mr. Bartlett.

And, yet, that wasn't all he had done. He paid those specialists to stay in the area and worked with local surgeons to make recovery and healing as complete as possible *for anyone else who had been caught in the destruction of Skull Junction.*

"I never suspected I had allowed my life to depend so crucially upon my wealth, or the lives of men who were so untrustworthy," Claiborne continued as Mr. Bartlett and he enjoyed being outside in the cool morning breeze.

Claiborne brought his hand to his mouth, embarrassed as he tried to fight back tears.

"I cry a lot," Andrew Bartlett told him. "I cry over the corruption I find in this government I serve—kickbacks to senators, dirty deals behind closed doors, drug parties, so much more. I decide to quit an average of five times a week, and then I realize that doing so would be to let down my president, who is a decent and honorable man, as well as my country."

"Thank you, Andrew," Claiborne said, wiping his eyes with a tissue. "Thank you for being as kind to me as you have been."

"But, Robert, *you* are the one who has these specialists here at the cost of hundreds of thousands of dollars."

"My original reason was to help *me,*" pointed out Claiborne.

"But it grew into something else. Be pleased with it. There's no basis for guilt. You're doing something wonderful."

"To deal with a nightmare created by brutal men on *my* payroll, two who caught so completely the wrong signals from me. But, you know as well as I do, that if I had been 'transmitting' something better, something finer, more decent, more loving—none of this would have happened."

Mr. Bartlett was silent for a moment.

"Andrew, are you all right?" Claiborne asked, concerned.

"Look, Robert. Look at who is coming to visit you."

Claiborne glanced in the direction Mr. Bartlett had been gazing.

Ryan and Chad were walking toward them.

And alongside the two teenagers was Brook-That-Sings.

"I don't want to see him," Claiborne protested. "I *can't* see him. Please, Andrew, please help me in this."

"It's a battle you have to fight, Robert. Once you've won this one, you'll be free. The joy that takes the place of your guilt will be a true miracle. Don't let this moment pass in defeat, my friend, don't let *that* happen!"

"Oh, Andrew, Andrew, after feeling so strong until now, after accumulating all the power I could, with so little else satisfying me, I . . . I feel so weak."

"Use that power, Robert. It's still there. No one's stolen it from you in your absence. You may have employed some scum, true, but you've also had loyal men and women working for you, people who think highly of you, and not out of fear, Robert, out of respect."

"How could they *ever* respect what I am?"

"What you *were,* friend, what you no longer are."

"It's not that simple, Andrew, it can't be that simple, Andrew."

"They've heard. The media has been covering what you've been doing for the victims. They see all this, and they realize a remarkable change is going on inside you, and all of them want to be there to welcome you back when you are able to resume your work."

"But they knew me before. Can't you see that? They saw my coldness, they saw my—."

A voice interrupted him.

"I heard what you were saying now, sir, and I'd like to give you a thought for consideration."

It was Brook-That-Sings.

Robert Claiborne blushed in embarrassment.

"Christians aren't perfect people," Brook-That-Sings told him. "We just realize that we have been forgiven. And in that forgiveness, we have found that there can be absolute peace."

The Indian bent down beside Claiborne and took one of the man's hands between his own.

"Your vice president is a believer," he said. "He got in touch with me just a couple of days ago."

"Jameson? Jameson's a Christian? I never noticed."

"There was much that you *didn't* notice, sir. But he never gave up. Jameson's been praying for you for a very long time, he tells me."

"But he should *despise* me," Claiborne replied. "He should want me out of the company and never have me involved with it again."

"That would be stealing it from you, sir. And as a Christian, that is something he *cannot* do."

Claiborne touched the bandages around his face and neck.

"There is more than one way to carry scars," he said softly.

"I'll help you," Brook-That-Sings told him. "I'll stay with you for as long as you need me."

"Your people have died because of the greedy example I set—," Claiborne was beginning to protest.

Brook-That-Sings smiled.

"Let me tell you a story," he said a hint of sadness in his voice. "Will you let me do that, Robert Claiborne?"

Claiborne nodded, as he closed his eyes and listened to the words his new friend spoke.

Brook-That-Sings told of an intense and brutal period when hatred consumed him day and night, driving him into troubled dreams that made sound sleeping just about impossible.

"I've got to admit that I felt the deepest, ugliest hatred for anyone who didn't have the same skin color that was mine," he admitted with some hesitation. "And I hated ClaStar most of all because it represented the white man's domination and exploitation."

He went on to say how one day a ten-year-old boy was dying in his arms.

"My people weren't able to afford the right medical treatment for him. And I knew what had caused his illness. So, then and there, I thought it would be a miracle if I didn't just go off and do to ClaStar something similar to what those two men ended up doing, but for a different reason.

"This boy was named Clear Sky. His eyes were the eyes of death, dark, blood-shot, filled with pain.

"Then, suddenly, something happened," Brook-That-Sings continued. "He started to smile. The death look passed. He reached up and wiped tears off my own cheeks."

For a moment, Brook-That-Sings couldn't continue.

Finally, he smiled a bit and went on, "Sorry about that. . . . Clear Sky spoke to me of Jesus then, of all that His death at Calvary meant. He said, 'Jesus doesn't want you to hate *anyone!*' His voice was so clear as he spoke, *so clear!* There was no mumbling, his words strong, a sparkle in his eyes, a peaceful look on his face.

"And then, oh Lord above, that . . . that little boy was gone. I still held his body, I hugged it close to me, trying somehow, I guess, to prevent his life from slipping away, but his soul already had gone on to be with the Savior he loved so very much."

Brook-That-Sings bowed his head for a moment, then looked up, his gaze meeting Robert Claiborne's.

"I love you, now, in the Lord, sir," he said warmly. "I can't turn my back on you. Jesus could have done so with someone like me, but He didn't. And now I want to pass that love along."

The two men reached out and embraced one another. To be sure, they weren't the only ones shedding tears that day.

# Seventeen

A great deal happened during the weeks and months that followed. Andrew Bartlett required more time to heal than anyone had anticipated. He was not able to return to the White House for many weeks. For much of that time, he could not be moved from the western hospital in which he originally had been confined.

As it turned out, Robert Claiborne's injuries, including his burns, were not as serious as Mr. Bartlett's. He was able to leave much sooner.

Able to, yes, but he stayed around until his new friend made the trip by plane back to Washington, D.C.

"You have a business to run, Bob, a very large business," Mr. Bartlett reminded him more than once. "You can't let it slide like this."

"I am *not* letting it slide, Andy," he replied. "I have spoken with several very good people who work for me, and they are doing fully as well as I ever did. A few weeks, one way or the other, matters not at all, my friend."

Finally, Andrew Bartlett was taken back to Washington, D.C. The vice president, himself, personally greeted Andy and his sons when they arrived in the nation's capital. That's when the three Bartletts learned something none of them would ever forget:

"Robert Claiborne has been engaged in quite a few stunning activities since he was released from the hospital."

"Like what?" Ryan asked.

"He has given that tribe of Native Americans a 50 percent stake in the Silver mine," the vice president said.

"Fifty percent?" Chad exclaimed.

"Exactly. And he has spent millions making sure all those poisons are going to be cleared away from the soil and water on the reservation. In addition, he has started work on construction of a massive transport system that carries water from a reservoir many miles away directly to the village."

The vice president was smiling.

"There's more?" Ryan and Chad both said at the same time.

"Oh, yes. He has started a regional school system specifically for Native American children. It will include everything from kindergarten through junior college providing highly subsidized tuitions for young people from all over the West. He has hired the very best teachers, provided the finest textbooks, audio-visual materials, athletic equipment, everything and anything necessary to make the education they secure there among the finest in the United States."

The vice president had stopped smiling, a quite different expression crossing his face.

"Robert Claiborne has terminal bone cancer," he said.

"He never said anything when we were at the hospital," Mr. Bartlett remarked, startled.

"He doesn't want pity," the vice president said. "Oh, Andy, so much has happened since you were in the fire."

Indeed . . . a great deal. . . .

As he had gotten stronger, Andrew Bartlett had tried, as much as possible, to keep himself informed about global events. There was that continuing civil war in Yugoslavia, new fighting in one of the more prosperous black-ruled nations in Africa; the outbreak of AIDS in one of the nations in the new Commonwealth of Independent States (formerly the U.S.S.R.); and so much more.

The vice president told him more, and yet with all the man said, nothing had as much impact on

Andrew Bartlett as what he had just learned about Robert Claiborne.

Shortly after he himself had fully recovered, Mr. Bartlett found out that Claiborne indeed had died, and attending a special funeral would be every member of the tribe that had almost been destroyed.

"He asked that he be buried on the reservation. "I can't go out there," Mr. Bartlett told his sons. "Would you go for me?"

"Sure!" they both said.

It didn't take them long to get ready. This time, transportation was on a commercial jet, not a government plane.

During the flight, Ryan and Chad talked about how quickly things had changed for them.

"A few months ago, we never knew anything like this would happen," Ryan remarked.

"We'd never heard of ClaStar Oil and Silver or Robert Claiborne or Brook-That-Sings," Chad agreed.

They felt sad but, also, they were happy—happy that no more innocent men, women, and children were dying on the reservation because of the greed of others. And they knew Claiborne's life had changed dramatically, that he had become a committed Christian.

They arrived at the airport out West just before dusk. Brook-That-Sings was waiting for them.

When they got to the village, they saw changes immediately—a large, new water tower; houses built of wood and brick instead of tepees and dirt huts; people no longer in rags but nice clothes; and a beautiful red brick church.

"Some of this has come from what we could accomplish with the money Robert Claiborne signed over to us," Brook-That-Sings told them. "Some of it has been constructed by his building crews, like the church and the water tower. Oh, how, life has been enriched for us, transformed, my brothers, and all by the grace of almighty God!"

Nobody was starving. Nobody was sick. Nobody had dirt on their faces and hopelessness in their eyes.

Ryan and Chad went to sleep on two separate waterbeds that night in a room that had central heating and air-conditioning.

And in the morning, a full breakfast was cooked for them.

A short while later, they were standing with Brook-That-Sings, Warm Sun, Tall Timber, Sweet Flower, and fifty others from the village, along with several hundred ClaStar employees, and nearly a thousand Native Americans from five states, as well as various politicians, news reporters, TV commentators, photographers, and others—a gathering that approached two thousand in number.

Brook-That-Sings was the last speaker. He delivered the eulogy, which he ended with: "My friend here was once my enemy; now he is my brother. Five months ago, I hated him; now, if he had lived and had needed me, I would have died for him if that would have spared his own life.

"Only Christ as Redeemer could have accomplished that. Only He as the Prince of Peace could have brought us together."

He closed his eyes for a moment, the emotions so strong.

Then Brook-That-Sings bent over the closed coffin and kissed the lid as he whispered, "Goodbye, my dear, beloved friend, good-bye . . . for now."

DON'T MISS THESE OTHER BARTLETT BROTHER ADVENTURES:

Sudden Fear

When Ryan Bartlett accidentally intercepts a computer message, he and his brother are stalked by terrorists, who plan to destroy a nuclear power plant. (ISBN 0–8499–3301–3)

Terror Cruise

The Bartlett family embarks on a Caribbean cruise that is supposed to be a time of rest and relaxation, but instead becomes a journey into terror. (ISBN 0–8499–3302–1)

The Frankenstein Project

While visiting a friend in the hospital, Ryan and Chad Bartlett come face to face with secret scientific experiments and mysterious children. (ISBN 0–8499–3303–X)

Forbidden River

The brothers find themselves in the midst of the war on drugs, with corruption and danger stretching from South America's Forbidden River to the U.S. Congress. (ISBN 0–8499–3304–8)

NOW AVAILABLE

Disaster Island

The Bartlett Brothers take a two-week trip to Hawaii—a trip they won in an essay competition. But the glamour comes to an abrupt end when the long-dormant volcano Diamond Head erupts, triggering other natural calamities that threaten to destroy the island of Oahu and everyone on it.

(ISBN 0–8499–3360–9)

AN EXCERPT

Though it was a dangerous goal for someone of his advanced age, the old man nevertheless wanted to climb Diamond Head before he died. He had lived in one area or another on Oahu all his life, but the the old man had no Hawaiian blood himself.

Because of this, in some respects, native Hawaiians would never really consider him anything but a *haole,* or foreigner. His neighbors through the years had almost always come from Hawaiian families. Their native roots went back a hundred years or, sometimes, quite a bit more.

But while he wasn't accepted nearly as much as he would have liked, he wasn't rejected outright either.

And now he had a chance to make a dream, a crazy, dangerous dream come true.

Diamond Head . . .

The old man had been over the famous volcano countless times by private plane, by helicopter, or by jetliner.

But his *final goal in life* was to climb it—to stand at the rim, to look down inside. And this morning, he had started up the side, which was covered with the rich plant life typical of most of the Hawaiian islands.

Heat.

The old man knew that such heat was unusual this early in the day.

His eyes opened wide!

The heat couldn't have been coming from the early morning sun so much as . . . from Diamond Head itself!

He decided, instantly, that that was impossible. The volcano had been extinct for a very long time.

The old man continued his climb by digging into the side of the familiar landmark, trying to dislodge as little dirt and plant life as possible.

He was halfway up when he began to feel very tired and stopped to rest.

Steam.

He saw it as he looked up at the rim.

Steam drifting over the edge.

What an odor, ugh! he remarked to himself.

He climbed a bit further.

Without warning, there was a scream.

The old man looked straight up, back at the rim.

Someone had fallen, a large body, covered with flames, heading directly toward him.

An instant later, the eruption started . . .

The gentle morning trade winds blew in off the clear, beautiful Pacific Ocean, as Ryan and Chad Bartlett sat on the colorful veranda of the Royal Hawaiian Hotel. This landmark building, with its long porch and bright pink color scheme, was set back from the main bustling shopping district of Waikiki Beach.

They were scheduled to stay in Honolulu for a few days of their two-week trip to Hawaii. With Honolulu as their temporary base, originally the two boys and their father had planned to drive around that island, Oahu, and then make arrangements to fly on to Kauai, Molokai, Maui, and The Big Island.

"First contest we ever won!" Chad exclaimed. "Too bad Dad was delayed by government business in South Africa."

"Well, it wasn't exactly a contest," Ryan replied as he drank from a tall, thin glass of some pink-colored guava juice he had learned to like a lot better than pineapple juice.

"Sure it was, Ryan. We entered. We won. Hey, what's the difference, anyway?"

All of a sudden, Ryan felt like the older brother.

"It was an essay co—," he started to say.

"See!" Chad proclaimed victoriously. "You were about to say contest, weren't you?"

"I was not," Ryan insisted.

"What then?"

"*Competition*, that's what."

"Yeah, yeah," Chad remarked teasingly. Then he saw a girl at the far end of the veranda where she also was enjoying the hotel's famous buffet breakfast.

Ryan noticed Chad's new interest and sighed to himself.

Showing through his tank top, his brother's muscular body along with his good looks always equaled girls. When I go around dressed in something like that, all I attract is pity, Ryan thought.

"She's cute," Chad stated the obvious, for if she weren't, he would hardly have been reacting to her the way he was.

"Go meet her. I know you're dying to," Ryan told him, feeling more irritable than he liked to admit.

This was especially odd in view of where they were. He loved Hawaii with its bright sun, its beautiful turquoise-blue ocean, and gentle breezes filled with all kinds of exotic scents.

Chad started to stand, then hesitated.

"Ryan?" he said.

"What is it?"

"You're acting strange."

"So what's different?"

"Seriously, are you all right?"

Ryan looked across at him.

"As in healthy and happy to be in paradise and all that? Sure, Chad, I guess I'm all right then."

"You're holding back. What is it?"

Ryan shivered a bit.

"You're cold?" Chad asked.

"It's 78 degrees now. How can I be cold?"

"Then why are you shivering?"

Ryan gulped. He loved his brother, but he seldom gave Chad much credit for real sensitivity in a situation like the present one. And now Chad was showing just that!

"Because I feel strange," Ryan admitted.

"Strange? Define strange."

"It's the same way I feel when Dad's in danger. It's hard to explain."

"I can see that. For someone who's usually so good with words, you're suddenly tongue-tied."

Ryan chuckled.

"I deserved that, I guess," he replied.

His gaze drifted toward Diamond Head, seen clearly in the distance.

Smoke!

Ryan sat up straight in his seat.

"Chad!" he said. "Look!"

"Look at what?" his brother asked dumbly.

"Diamond Head. Look at that smoke."

Chad now noticed it, too.

"Some brush on fire," he remarked. "It happens."

"I'm sure it does. But this is—."

His words were cut off by the sound of sirens.

Murmuring broke out among the various hotel guests who were also having breakfast on the veranda, a favorite spot for tourists. Right at the beach, it was surrounded by lush tropical semi-jungle. And it was hard to tell whether this had been its original state or if the jungle had been recreated. But the green and scarlet and yellow and pink were beautiful anyway.

Abruptly a short man who looked as though he easily could be of pure Hawaiian blood entered the veranda area, chattering excitedly, "*Wikiwiki, wikiwiki, wikiwiki!*"

Then he stood quietly for a moment, his face red, obviously embarrassed that he had slipped into his native tongue, which none of the visitors present could understand.

"I must ask you to follow me," he said, very, very nervously.

"What's the problem?" a large woman to his left demanded in a loud, hoarse voice.

"Someone from the Honolulu Police Department will explain."

"Police?" her male companion, also very big, asked. "Hey, what gives, mister?"

As though on cue, the ground rumbled beneath them.

"An earthquake?" Chad whispered to his brother.

"No, look!" Ryan replied, pointing toward Diamond Head.

That distant landmark seemed to be going through convulsions, shooting forth huge bursts of molten rock and sending it gushing over the sides of that familiarly-shaped crater, and down onto a—.

Another hotel at the base!

Since it was morning, many hotel guests were still asleep. When they were awakened by a roaring sound, and the massive shaking of the earth beneath them, they thought first of a strong earthquake.

Within a short while, lava had surrounded the main structure, which was ten stories high, and buried smaller ones on the hotel grounds.

Panic took over. In the lobby, people who had planned a day's tour of Oahu were heading frantically toward the nearest exits.

Most were too late. Lava came through the front entrance and through windows. Screaming men, women, and children ran for the stairs in a desperate race from the growing mass of molten rock.

Higher and higher they climbed. Higher and higher the lava rose. The careless ones slipped and fell into its red-hot mass. A handful made it to the top floor and hurried to windows and doorways that gave a view of their surroundings.

Diamond Head looked like a gigantic bathtub, but instead of water overflowing it, there were huge rivers of steamy, orange-red jello-thick molten rock.

Abruptly the building started to sway! Screams tore through the air. The middle of the floor literally became a bubbling pool of lava mixed with wood and concrete and steel.

Everyone ran in terror to the large outside patio. They could hear the sounds of helicopters, three large ones that had left Pearl Harbor minutes before.

Rope ladders were dropped down to the people. One by one, they started to climb up to the hovering copters—one at each end of the patio as well as another in the middle.

The elderly had the worst time of it. But others younger than they helped them, and soldiers pulled them inside each helicopter.

Seconds after the last guest had made it partway up, the entire hotel building collapsed, sending a burst of heat like a bomb blast against those still clinging to the ladders. The blast even rocked the copters, and the pilots struggled to keep from losing control.

Those who could bear to look saw below them a $50-million building disappear as though it were nothing more than a pasteboard movie set.

Buildings had sprung up over the years in nearly every direction around Diamond Head. This was prime real estate. Most were expensive residences, a large percentage costing well over a million dollars each.

All were destroyed. Families had little time to evacuate. They could not grab even any valuables. They lost everything they had.

Much later, in the mopping up aftermath of the eruption, great numbers of bewildered men, women, and children could be seen stumbling around, disbelieving, in the smoking wreckage.

Dozens who didn't make it were covered by the lava. But dozens more managed to find their way into the interior of Oahu, to settlements that had been erected by the original missionaries two hundred years earlier, and which were still maintained.

Among them were Ryan and Chad Bartlett and a little boy named Benny they had found as they were leaving the center of Honolulu and heading inland.

The three of them were huddled in an open field surrounded by jungle growth. Exotic plants were so densely packed together that hiking was almost impossible. This was a secluded part of Hawaii that had remained basically "pure" despite long years of wildly increasing building activity elsewhere on the island. In other areas residences and office structures now stood on land once covered with vegetation like this.

Ryan, Chad, and little Benny were not alone.

They had been joined by a dozen or more survivors, some of whom had found the spot inland by pure chance, others who were aware of it from either living on Oahu or as the result of previous visits to the island.

Ryan and Chad long had known about the old missionary camp. They had visited it before and knew how to get there. But it was quite some distance. At one point in their flight from Honolulu, neither of them knew if they would ever make it so far.

They had to get through the enormous crowds of people in cars or on motorcycles or, like themselves, being forced to run for it on foot.

At one point soon after they left the hotel, Ryan and Chad rescued a little boy even younger than Benny. The child would have been crushed to death if Chad hadn't grabbed him in time. The boy's parents failed to notice the crumbling storefront to their right.

"How can we ever thank you?" the young mother and father asked Chad.

They all agreed to keep in touch, if they survived this terrible disaster. Soon the parents and the little boy became separated from Ryan and Chad. They were caught up in a crowd going a different direction. Chad yelled after them, but they couldn't hear him because of the noise of falling buildings and the hysterical mob. Gripped by raging panic, many people were thinking far less clearly than they should have been.

Fortunately, after many trips to the Hawaiian Islands over the past few years, Ryan and Chad knew their way around Oahu. Others, however, in that huge mass of screaming and running and pushing bodies didn't have that advantage.

In fact, like the little boy and his mother and father, others were headed in the wrong direction, running blindly toward areas down-slope from

Diamond Head, which was exactly the direction the lava was flowing. But people thinking more clearly, like Ryan and Chad, were going inland toward the mountainous sections of Oahu!

"Listen!" a middle-aged man next to them shouted as he caught some news on his transistor radio.

"The eruption of once-dormant—not extinct, as many supposed—Diamond Head in the state of Hawaii has been joined by other catastrophic occurrences elsewhere in the world. There has been a major earthquake just outside Tokyo, Japan. Hundreds of millions of dollars in damage. The worst flood in more than a century has ravaged villages and towns all along the western coast of India.

"And within the continental United States, in the midst of farmlands all through the Midwest, locusts have returned in large numbers after an absence of many years.

"What we are seeing all over the world is like a scene from a biblical story of prophecy coming to pass right before our eyes!"

Ryan and Chad glanced at one another.

"Biblical prophecy," Ryan whispered. "Over public radio!"

"Yeah," his brother remarked. "I hate to say this, but I don't think it will do anything but add to the panic. And what about those who are converted now? How sincere will they be a year from now?"

"You're talking about foxhole Christianity," said Ryan.

"Exactly. People who turn to God only in time of trouble."

"But sometimes disaster can change a person forever. I guess we can only hope these people keep their faith when times are good," said Ryan.

Chad and Ryan had seen plenty of people praying during the mad dash they had made out Highway T, which was the main thoroughfare that cut directly down the center of Oahu.

Some of these people were knocked over and trampled on by other men and women who were thinking only of escape . . . escape from the lava that had reached the outskirts of Honolulu . . . escape from the toxic fumes in the air . . . escape from the spreading panic of which they all were a real part.

Other people were in prayer along the side of the highway itself.

That was where they had found Benny, kneeling beside a car that was a battered pile of twisted metal. They came up to him slowly. When the little boy realized that Ryan and Chad were next to him, he looked up, his expression brightening.

"I was asking God for help," he said, a little smile crossing his face. "Mom and Dad told me He listens real good."

At first Ryan and Chad assumed that the two bodies in the wrecked car must have been those of his parents.

Wrong.

As it turned out, Benny had become separated from his mother and father. And a young couple had hurriedly taken him into their car as they rushed for safety. Benny said they were going to help him find his parents.

Are we doomed?" the man with the radio asked. The expression on his face was full of fear as he turned to them.

"I don't know any more than you do, mister," Chad replied. "Nobody does except God Himself."

"But you were saying something about the Bible. I mean, I never paid much attention over the years. What does it say?"

"Pretty complicated to deal with in a few minutes," Ryan put in.

"Please try," the man asked urgently. "I'm interested. Maybe there are more like me here."

A murmur of assent.

Everyone else in that isolated spot had suddenly turned toward Ryan and Chad.

Ryan stood, feeling very uncomfortable being at the center of everybody's attention and wishing they had their father with them.

But they didn't.

Andrew Bartlett was in South Africa for meetings between the leaders of the warring tribes as well as the government and the two main black rebel groups. The meetings had run a few days longer than planned or he would have been with his sons in Hawaii.

Ryan felt that he and Chad were more alone now, in the middle of Hawaii, than just about any other time or place in their lives.

That included the time when Ryan accidently discovered a terrorist plot to blow up a nuclear power plant. Even then Andrew Bartlett managed to make it back to them, all the way from the Middle East.

And there was the huge and elegant *S. S. Oceanic*, a cruise ship that sank in shark-infested Caribbean waters, nearly taking the three of them with it. But at least they were all three together through that terrifying experience.

After nearly drowning, Andrew Bartlett was rescued, along with his sons, and finally another living nightmare ended, one that had started out as a relaxing vacation away from just the sort of thing that had happened anyway!

It was the same during their run-in with killers

associated with the Forbidden River drug cartel. Even in the midst of supposedly safe-and-secure Washington, D.C., their activities proved dangerous, just as Andrew Bartlett was starting his job as National Security Advisor.

And other times—Andrew Bartlett was always around or able to get to them before it was too late.

But, now, by the time he found out what had happened with Diamond Head, it could take a day or more to reach them.

For one thing, it might not be easy for anyone, including Andrew Bartlett, to get a plane on a moment's notice. Even those in high-level governmental circles had their limitations. And under no circumstances could any traveling time be cut from a flight beginning at the very bottom tip of Africa and extending all the way on to the Hawaiian Islands thousands of miles away. After all, airplanes could go just so fast.

We might be long dead by the time Dad arrives, Ryan told himself. *Even though we're now safe, no one here has any way of telling what might happen to us next.*

"Aren't you gonna tell us anything, kid?" a coarse voice broke into his thoughts.

He looked at the more than a dozen men and women, most of them tourists wearing bold-print, native-looking clothes.

All seemed desperate as they gathered in front of Ryan.

"Wait a minute!" a very overweight man grumbled out loud. "Why, he's just a scrawny, little wimp."

Wimp? He calls me a wimp, Ryan said to himself. *Better that than a sweaty overstuffed—!*

He had really become good at controlling his emotions. In fact, he didn't even lash back at the man. His temper was not as bad as it would have been a year ago in such a situation.

That energized Ryan. He uttered a quick, silent prayer for the Lord's guidance, then told his listeners what he had been able to learn about the part of biblical prophecy that dealt with upheaval on Planet Earth just prior to the Second Coming of Christ. . . .

It was obvious no one knew what to do, no leader as such had yet been appointed.

"Ryan," Chad whispered into his brother's ear. "It could be a problem, you know, just staying here."

"You want to go back down there?" Ryan asked. . . .

ABOUT THE AUTHOR

Award-winning author Roger Elwood is well known for his suspense-filled stories for both youth and adult readers. His twenty-six years of editing and writing experience include stories in *Today's Youth* and *Teen Life* magazines and a number of best-selling novels for Scholastic Book Clubs and Weekly Reader Book Clubs. He has also had titles featured by Junior Literary Guild and Science Fiction Book Club. Among his most outstanding adult books is *Angelwalk*, a winner of the Angel Award from Religion in Media.